The Little Mermaid

AND OTHER FAIRY TALES

HEIRLOOM EDITION

The Little Mermaid

AND OTHER FAIRY TALES

by
Hans
Christian
Andersen

ILLUSTRATED BY GUSTAV HJORTLUND

Translated from the Danish by R. P. Keigwin

PLATT & MUNK, *Publishers*   NEW YORK

This Heirloom Edition
is especially produced for
PLATT & MUNK, *Publishers*, New York 10, N. Y.
in Odense, Denmark, the birthplace of Hans Christian Andersen.

Library of Congress Catalog Card No. 63-14250

Contents

Hans Christian Andersen and his autograph.

Hans Christian Andersen

A BRIEF BIOGRAPHY

On New Year's Day, 1835, Hans Christian Andersen wrote to a woman friend: "I am now beginning some 'Fairy Tales for Children'; I shall try to win the future generation, you know!" and in a letter some time later he mentions that of "these stories, they say it is my Immortal Work."

These words from a young writer of 30 years of age sounded prophetic, and time justified them. Since the first edition was published, the stories have been printed over and over again. They are to be found throughout the whole world, translated into every important language.

The earliest of Hans Andersen's stories are founded on folk tales, but he did not simply tell the same story—he developed and recreated the folk story, and thus he differs from all other writers who have made use in their writings of material from old fairy tales.

About 1843, he changed over to his own original stories. "Now I tell stories with all my heart, get hold of an idea for the older folks, and then tell a story for the young folks, remembering all the time that father and mother often listen and we must give them something to think about, too! I have heaps of material, more than for any other kind of writing; it often seems to me as if every hoarding, every little flower is saying to me 'Look at me, just for a moment, and then my story will go right into you', and then, if I feel like it, I have the story."

That is what happened. The inspiration of the fairy tale could come from many places, from memories of childhood, or experiences on his travels, or from small episodes occurring by the way. Such fairy tale "seeds" are to be found scattered throughout his writings. They could lie buried in his mind for years. "They lay in my thoughts as a seed-corn, requiring only a flowing stream, a ray of sunshine, a drop from the cup of bitterness, for them to spring forth and burst into bloom."

Hans Andersen's fairy tale writings also differ from folk tales in the richness of their descriptions of nature. He had an exceptionally clear eye for the beauty of nature. Added to this, the stories ripple with humor. From first to last, one notices his wit in pointed and striking little situations: the Soldier's friends in "The Tinder Box", who deserted him when there were too many stairs to climb, the man in "Little Claus and Big Claus", who could not bear the sight of a parish clerk. The whole story can sometimes be a satire in itself as in "The Emperor's New Clothes" and "It's Absolutely True."

The fairy tale was the form of art which could completely reveal Hans Andersen's special talent, and it was the tool which he could so ably use to reveal common human weaknesses and also—when occasion arose—to send his personal bugbears a little message. It has been said that every story contains something of the poet's life-blood, and for this very reason they are undying.

From this it will be understood that there is a close connection between Hans Andersen's life story and his writing—the life story

Hans Christian Andersen's departure from Odense in 1819

Hans Christian Andersen being questioned for his student's examination in 1829.

he himself regarded as a fairy tale, the story of the poor boy who became a celebrated poet of world-wide fame, the story of the ugly duckling that became a beautiful swan.

He was born in Odense, in Denmark, on April 2, 1805. His home was a poor one. His father was a shoemaker, imaginative and romantic. Traits in the father's character were inherited by his son. His mother was a big strong woman, who did the best she could to keep the little home together, and when Hans Andersen looked back on his childhood home through the colored spectacles of memory it was enhanced in beauty. It was the circle of his childhood dreams. Here he played with the marionette theater which his father had made for him. He made costumes for the puppets himself, and on the ideas from the theater posters which were given to him, he wrote the plays. Only occasionally did he manage to go to the real theater, where a new world of make believe revealed itself to him.

Quite early he was known to be odd and different from other boys. He was "big and strange" like the ugly duckling and therefore he was an object of ridicule. He received only the scantiest of school learning, though in some subjects he was quite apt.

The Napoleonic Wars cast their shadow over his childhood home. His father succumbed to his urge for adventure and joined the army. Maybe financial circumstances compelled him to take this step. Hans Andersen's mother had to earn the daily bread by washing for people, and when his father returned home in a couple of years, he was so broken down in health that he died shortly afterwards. His mother married again, and the little Hans Andersen was left still more to himself.

He would sit by the Odense River for hours at a time, dreaming of strange lands, as he watched the foaming water streaming over the wheels of the water mill. Or he would sometimes accompany his grandmother to the hospital where poor elderly women sat spinning, and where he could listen to the tales they told, and also tell stories himself to impress them with his knowledge.

His childhood passed and he had to decide what he would be. His mother thought that he ought to learn a trade, and others advised him likewise. At that time, when there were very strong social distinctions, anything higher than this could not reasonably be contemplated for a boy who belonged to the lower strata of society.

But the boy's imagination carried him higher, and he made it clear to his family that he was going to be famous and that although he might have to go through terribly hard times, he was quite sure fame would come to him one day. The theater was the object of his ambition. He remembered his marionette theater, the plays he had been to at the Odense Theater, and people said that he had a nice voice. Down by the river, he had stood on a stone and sung in a loud voice to attract attention—in a garden nearby, there had been a party and several of the players from the Royal Theater had been there. The Royal Theater (he felt) must bring him the fame he strove for.

One day in September, 1819, the 14-year-old boy said good-bye to his mother and grandmother and set off for Copenhagen. He suffered hardships in the large unfamiliar city, but he managed to get taken as a pupil at the theater to which he gave—then and always—an unhappy devotion.

But he was not to be an actor. His talent did not lie in this direction,

Hans Christian Andersen with a friend in Naples in 1834.

Hans Christian Andersen reading fairy tales to the Collin family.

and there came a day, after a couple of years at the theater, when he was discharged from its service.

In the ordinary course of events one would think that Hans Andersen would now be quite helpless, and destined to sink to the bottom of society. He had no education or training that could help him to earn a living. He had not a single relation who could help him. But he had a burning faith in God who was sure to come to his aid, and he was determined to win through. It must have been this strange self-confidence that arrested the attention of influential people, and gained for him admission to circles which would otherwise have been closed to him.

That one of the directors of the Royal Theater, Jonas Collin, interested himself in Andersen was of the greatest significance to his future career. He recognized that, first and foremost, it was necessary to give Hans Christian Andersen the knowledge and education which he lacked. He arranged for him to go to a Latin School. Steady work was not in Andersen's line, neither was it pleasant for him to sit side by side with much younger boys in a junior class. Again his schoolfellows found him "big and strange." After many trials and troubles, however, he managed to pass his student's examination in 1829 and he could now devote himself to the art of writing, which he had already, during the years of hardship, practiced in secret.

He began as a lyrical and humorous poet, as in "The Dying Child" which was printed anonymously in 1827 and gained for him a certain fame. The humorous story "Walking Tour from Holmens Canal to Østpynten of Amager" made a name for him.

During one of his visits to Funen in 1830, he fell in love with the daughter of a rich merchant, Riborg Voigt, but she was already engaged. The outcome of this unhappy love affair was a collection of love poems, which in beauty are comparable with the finest in Danish literature. To console himself, he went in 1831 on his first trip abroad—to Northern Germany—which he describes in the book "Rambles in the Harz Mountains." This first travel book revealed the rare powers of observation which were characteristic of all his later work.

So he started on the course which he was to follow throughout his life. A new era in his life was his journey to Italy 1833–34, which bore fruit in "The Improvisatore." This book was translated into German and English which introduced him to a European public. The book was published in 1835, and the same year the first fairy tales came out, but Hans Andersen himself regarded these as a mere bagatelle. He thought that the novel was the literary form which suited him best, and in the following years he produced a number of works which have now faded in the light of his fairy tales, but they have a vigor all their own and they are filled with vivid scenes from his life and travels.

He never lost interest in the theater. He revised the works of foreign authors, was successful in getting several accepted for performance at the Royal Theater, wrote original plays, some of them melodramatic and of little worth; others—in which he adopted a popular tone and cast over them the brilliance of his make believe— won favor among his contemporaries.

The fairy tale, however, came to be the crowning glory of his work. Every year a small booklet of these stories was published, each

Hans Christian Andersen with other guests at Nysø, a Zealand town south of Copenhagen.

The great Swedish singer, Jenny Lind, singing before the Hereditary Archduke and Hans Christian Andersen at Weimar, Germany in 1846.

perfect in form and content—superb masterpieces, which have made his name famed far beyond his native land.

It is said that the story of "The Ugly Duckling" is the life story of Hans Andersen. With equal truth it can be said that the story "The Fir Tree" expresses the steady yearning after change which lay deep-seated in the soul of Hans Andersen.

Hans Andersen was never married. He was infatuated with Jonas Collin's daughter Louise. He was passionately in love with the great Swedish singer, Jenny Lind, whom he met in the forties in Copenhagen and in Berlin, but he never had a home except such as he found among his many good friends, first and foremost in the home of the Collin family. It was this home he sought with his joys and sorrows, and here he was looked upon as one of the family.

In Hans Andersen's Museum in Odense we can see his traveling equipment, his bag, walking stick and umbrella. These are symbolic of him. Travel was a vital necessity to him—seeking contact with other people in his native land and abroad.

From the middle of the thirties, he was a regular and welcome guest at Danish castles and manor houses, where his stories were listened to with joy, and where he himself delighted in the beautiful surroundings and gathered inspiration for his writings. These sojourns were interrupted by his journeys abroad, which, all in all, occupied about nine years of his life. These journeys also brought him into easy and familiar contact with important personalities.

He often went to Germany, where he received great hospitality at the Royal Courts, particularly at Weimar. He went to England in 1847 and 1857, when he made friends with Charles Dickens. In fact, he went to all countries in Europe. Italy was his favorite country. He felt quite at home wandering in the streets of Rome, and rejoiced in the blue Mediterranean and the brilliant sunshine. He had friends in Switzerland and was impressed by the magnificent scenery to which he gives expression in the story "The Ice Maiden." In 1840–41, he made the long journey to Greece and Turkey and reproduced his experiences in the breezy and delightful travel tale "A Poet's Bazaar." Spain, Portugal, Belgium and Holland, Sweden and Norway he visited one or more times. "To travel is to live" was one of his favorite sayings. He made notes of his impressions, drew sketches of the landscape and houses he saw, all with the intention of letting them settle down in his mind, to be reproduced one day, in his writings.

In the winter, when he was back home again in Copenhagen, he had to keep the connections he had made, and wrote letters to his friends. He wrote innumerable letters as rich and as entertaining as his stories, and they provide the best sources of information about his life.

Hans Andersen had a very sensitive nature. He took criticism very badly and suffered from a sense of bitterness when many Danish critics, quite justly, raised objections to his dramatic works and found fault with his novels. It was some time before he understood that it was his fairy tales that raised him above contemporary writers. Yet he was deeply touched and warmed in spirit when he found acknowledgment. He felt that his talent was more appreciated abroad, and that there people were less inclined to notice his shortcomings.

The truth is, however, that his native land shed its appreciation on him in great measure. He enjoyed the favor and grace of the

Torchlight procession in honor of Hans Christian Andersen at Odense in 1867.

Royal Family, he was honored with titles and orders, and, as the years passed, his bitterness gave way to a profound feeling of fellowship with his native land, a feeling which matured to still greater fullness after Denmark's defeat in the war with Germany in 1864. In 1867 he was honored with the Freedom of the City of his native town. Odense was illuminated, a torchlight procession was made for him, and then he felt how wonderfully God had guided him; that his life, indeed, was as a fairy tale, rich and happy.

The last years of his life were marked by increasing illness, and only with difficulty could he go on his travels. He had, in Copenhagen, become closely attached to a wholesale merchant, M. G. Melchior, whose wife cared tenderly for him, and in Melchior's home he died on August 4, 1875.

Other writers have, during their lifetime, attained similar renown, but the works of few authors live beyond the period of their creation. Hans Andersen's stories have done this. They were written for children, but it was Andersen's hope that their parents would also listen, and several of his stories are more for grownups than for children—for only the mature can understand the depth of these writings. Today, almost a century after his death, the name of Hans Christian Andersen shines among the most illustrious names of world literature, and his stories remain just as fresh and vigorous, for they are concerned with the emotions of mankind throughout the ages and are thus raised above the limitations of Time and Place.

Svend Larsen

The Little Mermaid

Far out at sea the water's as blue as the petals of the loveliest cornflower, and as clear as the purest glass; but it's very deep, deeper than any anchor can reach. Many church steeples would have to be piled up one above the other to reach from the bottom of the sea to the surface. Right down there live the sea people.

Now you mustn't for a moment suppose that it's a bare white sandy bottom. Oh, no. The most wonderful trees and plants are growing down there, with stalks and leaves that bend so easily that they stir at the very slightest movement of the water, just as though they were alive. All the fishes, big ones and little ones, slip in and out of the branches just like birds in the air up here. Down in the deepest part of all is the Sea King's palace. Its walls are made of coral, and the long pointed windows of the clearest amber; but the roof is made of cockle-shells that open and shut with the current. It's a pretty sight, for in each shell is a dazzling pearl; any single one of them would be a splendid ornament in a Queen's crown.

The Sea King down there had been a widower for some years, but his old mother kept house for him. She was a clever woman, but proud of her noble birth; that's why she went about with twelve oysters on her tail, while the rest of the nobility had to put up with only six. But apart from that, she was deserving of special praise, because she was so fond of the little Sea Princesses, her grandchildren. They were six pretty children, but the youngest was the loveliest of them all. Her skin was as clear and delicate as a rose petal, her eyes were as blue as the deepest lake, but like the others she had no feet; her body ended in a fish's tail.

All the long day they could play down there in the palace, in the great halls where living flowers grew out of the walls. The fishes would swim in to them, just as with us the swallows fly in when we open the windows; but the fishes swam right up to the little Princesses, fed out of their hands, and let themselves be patted.

Outside the palace was a large garden with trees of deep blue and fiery red; the fruit all shone like gold, and the flowers like a blazing fire with stalks and leaves that were never still. The soil itself was the finest sand, but blue like a sulphur flame. Over everything down there lay a strange blue gleam; you really might have thought you were standing high up in the air with nothing to see but sky above and below you,

rather than that you were at the bottom of the sea. When there was a dead calm you caught a glimpse of the sun, which looked like a purple flower pouring out all light from its cup.

Each of the small Princesses had her own little plot in the garden, where she could dig and plant at will. One of them gave her flower bed the shape of a whale, another thought it nicer for hers to look like a little mermaid; but the youngest made hers quite round like the sun, and would only have flowers that shone red like it. She was a curious child, silent and thoughtful; and when the other sisters decorated their gardens with the most wonderful things they had got from sunken ships, she would have nothing but the rose-red flowers that were like the sun high above, and a beautiful marble statue. It was the statue of a handsome boy, hewn from the clear white stone and come down to the bottom of the sea from a wreck. Beside the statue she planted a rose-red weeping willow, which grew splendidly and let its fresh foliage droop over the statue right down to the blue sandy bottom. Here the shadow took on a violet tinge and, like the branches, was never still; roots and treetop looked as though they were playing at kissing each other.

Nothing pleased her more than to hear about the world of humans up above the sea. The old grandmother had to tell her all she knew about ships and towns, people and animals. One thing especially surprised her with its beauty, and this was that the flowers had a smell—at the bottom of the sea they hadn't any—and also that the woods were green and the fishes you saw in among the branches could sing as clearly and prettily as possible. It was the little birds that the grandmother called fishes; otherwise, never having seen a bird, the small Sea Princesses would never have understood her.

"As soon as you are fifteen," the grandmother told them, "you shall be allowed to rise to the surface, and to sit in the moonlight on the rocks and watch the great ships sailing past; you shall see woods and towns." That coming year one of the sisters was to have her fifteenth birthday, but the rest of them—well, they were each one year younger than the other; so the youngest of them had a whole five years to wait before she could rise up from the bottom and see how things are with us. But each promised to tell the others what she had seen and found most interesting on the first day; for their grandmother didn't really tell them enough—there were so many things they were longing to hear about.

None of them was so full of longing as the youngest—the very one who had most time to wait and was so silent and thoughtful. Many a night she stood at the open window and gazed up through the dark-blue water, where the fishes frisked their tails and fins. She could see the moon and the stars, though it's true their light was rather pale; and yet through the water they looked much larger than they do to us, and if ever a kind of black cloud went gliding along below them, she knew it was either a whale swimming above her or else a vessel with many passengers; these certainly never imagined that a lovely little mermaid was standing beneath and stretching up her white hands toward the keel of their ship.

By now the eldest Princess was fifteen and allowed to go up to the surface.

When she came back, she had a hundred things to tell; but the loveliest, she said, was to lie in the moonlight on a sandbank in a calm sea and there, close in to the shore, to look at the big town where the lights were twinkling like a hundred stars; to listen to the sound of

music and the noise and clatter of carts and people; to see all the towers and spires on the churches and hear the bells ringing. And just because she couldn't get there, it was this above everything that she longed for.

Oh, how the youngest sister drank it all in! And, when later in the evening she stood at the open window and gazed up through the dark-blue water, she thought of the big town with all its noise and clatter, and then she seemed to catch the sound of the church bells ringing down to her.

The following year, the second sister was allowed to go up through the water and swim wherever she liked. She came to the surface just as the sun was setting, and that was the sight she found most beautiful. The whole sky had looked like gold, she said, and the clouds—well, she just couldn't describe how beautiful they were as they sailed, all crimson and violet, over her head. And yet, much faster than they, a flock of wild swans flew like a long white veil across the water where the sun was setting. She swam off in that direction, but the sun sank, and its rosy light was swallowed up by sea and cloud.

The year after that, the third sister went up. She was the boldest of them all, and she swam up a wide river that flowed into the sea. She saw delightful green slopes with grapevines; manors and farms peeped out among magnificent woods; she heard all the birds singing; and the sun was so hot that she often had to dive under the water to cool her burning face. In a small cove she came upon a swarm of little human children splashing about quite naked in the water. She wanted to play with them, but they ran away terrified, and a little black animal came up; it was a dog. She had never seen a dog before. It barked at her so dreadfully that she got frightened and made for the open sea.

But never could she forget the magnificent woods, the green slopes and the darling children, who could swim on the water although they had no fishes' tails.

The fourth sister was not so bold. She kept far out in the wild waste of ocean, and told them that was just what was so wonderful: you could see for miles and miles around you, and the sky hung above like a big glass bell. She had seen ships, but a long way off, looking like sea gulls. The jolly dolphins had been turning somersaults, and enormous whales had spurted up water from their nostrils, so that they seemed to be surrounded by a hundred fountains.

And now it was the turn of the fifth sister. Her birthday happened to come in winter, and so she saw things that the others hadn't seen the first time. The sea appeared quite green, and great icebergs were floating about; they looked like pearls, she said, and yet were much larger than the church towers put up by human beings. They were to be seen in the most fantastic shapes, and they glittered like diamonds. She had sat down on one of the biggest, and all the ships gave it a wide berth as they sailed in terror past where she sat with her long hair streaming in the wind. But late in the evening the sky became overcast with clouds; it lightened and thundered, as the dark waves lifted the great blocks of ice right up, so that they flashed in the fierce red lightning. All the ships took in sail, and, amidst the general horror and alarm, she sat calmly on her floating iceberg and watched the blue lightning zigzag into the glittering sea.

The first time one of the sisters went up to the surface, she would always be delighted to see so much that was new and beautiful; but afterwards, when they were older and could go up as often as they liked, it no longer interested them; they longed to be back again, and

when a month had passed they said that, after all, it was nicest down below—it was such a comfort to be home.

Often of an evening the five sisters used to link arms and float up together out of the water. They had lovely voices, more beautiful than any human voice; and when a gale sprang up threatening shipwreck, they would swim in front of the ships and sing tempting songs of how delightful it was at the bottom of the sea. And they told the sailors not to be afraid of coming down there, but the sailors couldn't make out the words of their song; they thought it was the noise of the gale, nor did they ever see any of the delights the mermaids promised, because when the ship sank the crew were drowned, and only as dead men did they come to the palace of the Sea King.

When of an evening the sisters floated up through the sea like this, arm in arm, their little sister stayed back all alone gazing after them. She would have cried, only a mermaid hasn't any tears, and so she suffers all the more.

"Oh, if only I were fifteen!" she said. "I'm sure I shall love that world up there and the people who live in it."

And then at last she was fifteen.

"There, now you'll soon be off our hands," said her grandmother, the old Dowager Queen. "Come now, let me dress you up like your sisters!" and she put a wreath of white lilies on her hair, but every petal of the flower was half a pearl. And the old lady made eight big oysters nip tight on to the Princess' tail to show her high rank.

"Oo! that hurts," said the little mermaid.

"Yes," said the grandmother, "one can't have beauty for nothing."

How she would have liked to shake off all this finery and put away the heavy wreath! The red flowers in her garden suited her much better, but she didn't dare make any change. "Good-bye," she said, and went up through the water as light and clear as a bubble.

The sun had just set, as she put her head up out of the sea, but the clouds had still a gleam of rose and gold; and up in the pale pink sky the evening star shone clear and beautiful. The air was soft and fresh, and the sea dead calm. A large three-masted ship was lying there, with only one sail hoisted because not a breath of wind was stirring, and sailors were lolling about in the rigging and on the yards. There was music and singing, and as it grew dark hundreds of lanterns were lit that, with their many different colors, looked as if the flags of all nations were flying in the breeze.

The little mermaid swam right up to the porthole of the cabin and, every time she rose with the wave's swell, she could see through the clear glass a crowd of splendidly dressed people; but the handsomest of them all was a young Prince with large dark eyes. He couldn't have been much more than sixteen; it was his birthday, and that's why there was all this festivity. As the young Prince came out on to the deck where sailors were dancing, over a hundred rockets swished up into the sky—and broke into a glitter like broad daylight. That frightened the little mermaid, and she dived down under the water; but she quickly popped up her head again, and look! it was just as if all the stars in heaven were falling down on her. Never had she seen such fireworks. Great suns went spinning around, gorgeous fire fishes swerving into the blue air, and all this glitter was mirrored in the clear still water. On board the ship herself it was so light that you could make out every little rope, let alone the passengers. Oh, how handsome the young Prince was; he shook hands with the sailors, he laughed and smiled, while the music went floating out into the loveliness of the night.

It grew late, but the little mermaid couldn't take her eyes off the ship and the beautiful Prince. The colored lanterns were put out, the rockets no longer climbed into the sky, and the cannon were heard no more; but deep down in the sea there was a mumbling and a rumbling. Meanwhile the mermaid stayed on the water, rocking up and down so that she could look into the cabin. But the ship now gathered speed; one after another her sails were spread. The waves increased, heavy clouds blew up, and lightning flashed in the distance. Yes, they were in for a terrible storm; so the sailors took in their sails, as the great ship rocked and scudded through the raging sea. The waves rose higher and higher like huge black mountains, threatening to bring down the mast, but the ship dived like a swan into the trough of the waves and then rode up again on their towering crests. The little mermaid thought, why, it must be fun for a ship to sail like that—but the crew didn't. The vessel creaked and cracked, the stout planks crumpled up under the heavy pounding of the sea against the ship, the mast snapped in the middle like a stick, and then the ship gave a lurch to one side as the water came rushing into the hold. At last the little mermaid realized that they were in danger; she herself had to look out for the beams and bits of wreckage that were drifting on the water. One moment it was so pitch dark that she couldn't see a thing, but then when the lightning came it was so bright that she could make out everyone on board. It was now a case of each man for himself. The young Prince was the one she was looking for and, as the ship broke up, she saw him disappear into the depths of the sea. Just for one moment she felt quite pleased, for now he would come down to her; but then she remembered that humans can't live under the water and that only as a dead man could he come down to her father's palace. No, no, he mustn't die. So she swam in among the drifting beams and planks, with no thought for the danger of being crushed by them; she dived deep down and came right up again among the waves, and at last she found the young Prince. He could hardly swim any longer in the heavy sea; his arms and legs were beginning to tire, the fine eyes were closed; he would certainly have drowned if the little mermaid had not come. She held his head above water and then let the waves carry her along with him wherever they pleased.

By morning the gale had quite gone; not the smallest trace of the ship was to be seen. The sun rose red and glowing out of the water and seemed to bring life to the Prince's cheeks, but his eyes were still shut. The mermaid kissed his fine high forehead and smoothed back his dripping hair. He was like the marble statue down in her little garden; she kissed him again and wished that he might live.

Presently she saw the mainland in front of her, high blue mountains with the white snow glittering on their peaks like nestling swans. Down by the shore were lovely green woods and, in front of them, a church or a convent—she wasn't sure which, but anyhow a building. Lemon and orange trees were growing in the garden, and tall palm trees in front of the gate. At this point the sea formed a little inlet, where the water was quite smooth but very deep close in to the rock where the fine white sand had silted up. She swam here with the handsome Prince and laid him on the sand with his head carefully pillowed in the warm sunshine.

Now there was a sound of bells from the large white building, and a number of young girls came through the garden. So the little mermaid swam further out behind some large boulders that were sticking out

44

of the water and covered her hair and breast with seafoam, so that her face wouldn't show; and then she watched to see who would come to the aid of the unfortunate Prince.

It wasn't long before a young girl came along. She seemed quite frightened, but only for a moment; then she fetched several others, and the mermaid saw the Prince come around and smile at those about him; but no smile came out to her, for of course he didn't know she had rescued him. She felt so sad that, when he was taken away into the large building, she dived down sorrowfully into the sea and went back to her father's palace.

Silent and thoughtful as she had always been, she now became much more so. Her sisters asked her what she had seen on her first visit to the surface, but she wouldn't say.

Many a morning and many an evening she rose up to where she had left the Prince. She saw the fruit in the garden ripen and be gathered, she saw the snow melt on the peaks, but she never saw the Prince, and so she always turned back more despondent than ever. Her one comfort was to sit in the little garden with her arms around the beautiful marble statue which was so like the Prince. She never looked after her flowers, and they grew into a sort of wilderness, out over the paths, and braided their long stalks and leaves on to the branches of the trees, until the light was quite shut out.

At last she could keep it to herself no longer, but told one of her sisters; and immediately all the rest got to know, but nobody else— except a few other mermaids who didn't breathe a word to any but their nearest friends. One of these was able to say who the Prince was; she, too, had seen the party that was held on board the ship, and knew where he came from and whereabouts his kingdom was.

"Come on, little sister!" said the other Princesses. And with arms round each other's shoulders they rose in one line out of the sea, just in front of where the Prince's castle stood. It was built of a glistening stone of pale yellow with great flights of marble steps; one of these led straight into the sea. Splendid gilt domes curved above the roof, and between the pillars that went right around the building were lifelike sculptures in marble. Through the clear glass in the tall windows you could see into the most magnificent rooms; these were hung with sumptuous silk curtains and tapestries and their walls were covered with large paintings that were a delight to the eye. In the middle of the biggest room was a huge splashing fountain; its spray was flung high up to the glass dome in the ceiling, through which the sun shone down on to the water and the beautiful plants growing in the great pool.

Now she knew where he lived, and many an evening and many a night she would come to the surface at that spot. She swam much closer to the shore than any of the others had ever dared. She even went up the narrow creek under the fine marble balcony that threw its long shadow across the water. Here she would sit and gaze at the young Prince, who imagined he was quite alone in the clear moonlight.

Often in the evening she saw him go out to the strains of music in his splendid vessel that was dressed with flags. She peeped out from among the green rushes and, when the wind caught her long silvery veil and someone saw it, they fancied it was a swan spreading its wings.

On many nights, when the fishermen were at sea with their torches, she heard them speaking so well of the young Prince, and that made her glad she had saved his life when he drifted about half-dead on the waves; and she thought of how closely his head had rested on her bosom and how lovingly she had kissed him. But he knew nothing whatsoever about that, never even dreamed she existed.

Fonder and fonder she became of human beings, more and more she longed for their company. Their world seemed to her to be so much larger than her own. You see, they could fly across the ocean in ships, climb the tall mountains high above the clouds; and the lands they owned stretched with woods and meadows further than her eyes could see. There was so much she would have liked to know, but her sisters couldn't answer all her questions, and so she asked the old grandmother, for she knew all about the upper world—as she so aptly called the countries above the sea.

"If people don't drown," asked the little mermaid, "can they go on living forever? Don't they die, as we do down here in the sea?"

"Yes, yes," said the old lady, "they, too, have to die; their lifetime is even shorter than ours. We can live for three hundred years, but when our life here comes to an end we merely turn into foam on the water; we haven't even a grave down here among those we love. We've no immortal soul; we shall never have another life. We're like the green rush—once it's been cut it can't grow green again. But human beings have a soul which lives forever; still lives after the body is turned to dust. The soul goes climbing up through the clear air, up till it reaches the shining stars. Just as we rise up out of the sea and look at the countries of human beings, so they rise up to beautiful unknown regions—ones we shall never see."

"Why haven't we got an immortal soul?" the little mermaid asked sadly. "I would give the whole three hundred years I have to live, to become for one day a human being and then share in that heavenly world."

"You mustn't go worrying about that," said the grandmother. "We're much happier and better off here than the people who live up there."

"So then I'm doomed to die and float like foam on the sea, never to hear the music of the waves or see the lovely flowers and the red sun. Isn't there anything at all I can do to win an immortal soul?"

"No," said the old lady. "Only if a human being loved you so much that you were more to him than father and mother—if he clung to you with all his heart and soul, and let the priest put his right hand in yours as a promise to be faithful and true here and in all eternity— then his soul would flow over into your body and you, too, would get a share in human happiness. He would give you a soul and yet keep his own. But that can never happen. The very thing that's so beautiful here in the sea, your fish's tail, seems ugly to people on the earth; they know so little about it that they have to have two clumsy supports called legs, in order to look nice."

That made the little mermaid sigh and look sadly at her fish's tail.

"We must be content," said the old lady. "Let's dance and be gay for the three hundred years we have to live—that's a good time, isn't it?—then one can have one's fill of sleep in the grave all the more pleasantly afterwards. Tonight we're having a Court ball."

That was something more magnificent than we ever see on the earth. In the great ballroom walls and ceiling were made of thick but quite clear glass. Several hundred enormous shells, rose-red and grass-green, were ranged on either side, each with a blue-burning flame which lit up the whole room and, shining out through the walls, lit up the sea outside as well. Countless fishes, big and small, could be seen swimming toward the glass walls; the scales on some of them shone purple-red, and on others like silver and gold . . . Through the middle of the ballroom flowed a wide running stream, on which mermen and mermaids danced to their own beautiful singing. No human beings have voices so lovely. The little mermaid sang the most sweetly of them all, and they clapped their hands for her, and for a moment there was joy in her heart, for she knew that she had the most beautiful voice on earth or sea. But then her thoughts soon returned to the world above her; she couldn't forget the handsome Prince and her sorrow at not possessing, like him, an immortal soul. So she crept out of her father's palace and, while all in there was song and merriment, she sat grieving in her little garden. Suddenly she caught the sound of a horn echoing down through the water, and she thought, "Ah, there he is, sailing up above—he whom I love more than father or mother, he who is always in my thoughts and in whose hands I would gladly place the happiness of my life. I will dare anything to win him and an immortal soul. While my sisters are dancing there in my father's palace, I will go to the sea witch; I've always been dreadfully afraid of her, but perhaps she can help me and tell me what to do."

So the little mermaid left her garden and set off for the place where the witch lived, on the far side of the roaring whirlpools. She had never been that way before. There were no flowers growing, no sea grass, nothing but the bare gray sandy bottom stretching right up to the whirlpools, where the water went swirling around like roaring mill wheels and pulled everything it could clutch down with it to the depths.

She had to pass through the middle of these battering eddies in order to get to the sea witch's domain; and here, for a long stretch, there was no other way than over hot bubbling mud—the witch called it her swamp. Her house lay behind it in the middle of an extraordinary wood. All the trees and bushes were polyps, half animals and half plants. They looked like hundred-headed snakes growing out of the earth; all the branches were long slimy arms with supple wormlike fingers, and joint by joint from the root up to the very tip they were continuously on the move. They wound themselves tight around everything they could clutch hold of in the sea, and they never let go. The little mermaid was terribly scared as she paused at the edge of the wood. Her heart was throbbing with fear; she nearly turned back. But then she remembered the Prince and the human soul, and that gave her courage. She wound her long flowing hair tightly around her head, so that the polyps shouldn't have that to clutch her by, she folded both her hands across her breast and darted off just as a fish darts through the water, in among the hideous polyps which reached out for her with their supple arms and fingers. She noticed how each of them had something they had caught, held fast by a hundred little arms like hoops of iron. White skeletons of folk who had been lost at sea and had sunk to the bottom looked out from the arms of the polyps. Ship's rudders and chests were gripped tight, skeletons of land animals, and—most horrible of all—a small mermaid whom they had caught and throttled.

Now she came to a large slimy open space in the wood where big fat water snakes were frisking about and showing their hideous whitish-yellow bellies. In the middle was a house built of the bones of human folk who had been wrecked.

There sat the sea witch, letting a toad feed out of her mouth, just as we might let a little canary come and peck sugar. She called the horrible fat water snakes her little chicks and allowed them to sprawl about her great spongy bosom.

"I know well enough what you're after," said the sea witch. "How stupid of you! Still, you shall have your way, and it'll bring you into misfortune, my lovely Princess. You want to get rid of your fish's tail and in its place have a couple of stumps to walk on like a human being, so that the young Prince can fall in love with you and you can win him and an immortal soul"—and with that the witch gave such a loud repulsive laugh that the toad and the snakes fell to the ground and remained sprawling there. "You've just come at the right time," said the witch. "Tomorrow, once the sun's up, I couldn't help you for another year. I shall make you a drink, and before sunrise you must swim to land, sit down on the shore and drink it up. Then your tail will divide in two and shrink into what humans call 'pretty legs'. But it'll hurt; it'll be like a sharp sword going through you. Everyone who sees you will say you are the loveliest human child they have ever seen.

You will keep your graceful movements—no dancer can glide so lightly—but every step you take will feel as if you were treading on a sharp knife, enough to make your feet bleed. Are you ready to bear all that? If you are, I'll help you."

"Yes," said the little mermaid, and her voice trembled; but she thought of her Prince and the prize of an immortal soul.

"Still, don't forget this," said the witch, "once you have a human shape, you can never become a mermaid again. You can never go down through the water to your sisters and to your father's palace; and if you don't win the Prince's love, so that he forgets father and mother for you and always has you in his thoughts and lets the priest join your hands together to be man and wife, then you won't get an immortal soul. The first morning after the Prince marries someone else, your heart must break and you become foam on the water."

"I'm ready," said the little mermaid, pale as death.

"Then there's me to be paid," said the witch, "and you're not getting my help for nothing. You have the loveliest voice of all down here at the bottom of the sea. With that voice, no doubt, you think to enchant him; but that voice you shall hand over to me. I demand the best that you have for me to make a rich drink. You see, I have to give you my own blood, in order that the drink may be as sharp as a two-edged sword."

"But if you take my voice," said the little mermaid, "what shall I have left?"

"Your lovely form," said the witch, "your graceful movements, and your speaking eyes. With those you can so easily enchant a human heart ... Well, where's your spunk? Put out your little tongue and let me cut it off in payment; then you shall be given the potent mixture."

"Go on, then," said the little mermaid, and the witch put the kettle on for brewing the magic drink. "Cleanliness before everything," she said, as she scoured out the kettle with a bundle of snakes she had knotted together. Next, she scratched her breast and let her black blood drip down into the kettle; the steam took on the weirdest shapes, terrifying to look at. The witch kept popping fresh things into the kettle, and when it boiled up properly it sounded like a crocodile in tears. At last the brew was ready; it looked like the clearest water.

"There you are!" said the witch and cut off the little mermaid's tongue; she was now dumb and could neither sing nor speak.

"If the polyps should catch hold of you, as you go back through the wood," said the witch, "throw but a single drop of this drink on them, and their arms and fingers will burst into a thousand pieces." But the little mermaid had no need to do that. The polyps shrank from her in terror when they saw the dazzling drink that shone in her hand like a glittering star. So she quickly came through the wood, the swamp and the roaring whirlpools.

She could see her father's palace; the lights were out in the great ballroom. They were all certain to be asleep in there by this time; but she didn't anyhow dare to look for them, now that she was dumb and was going to leave them forever. She felt as if her heart must break for grief. She stole into the garden, picked one flower from each of her sisters' flower beds, blew a thousand finger kisses toward the palace, and rose then through the dark-blue sea.

The sun was not yet up, as she sighted the Prince's castle and climbed the magnificent marble steps. The moon was shining wonderfully clear. The little mermaid drank the sharp burning potion, and it was as if a two-edged sword pierced through her delicate body—she

fainted and lay as though dead. Then the sun, streaming over the sea, woke her up, and she felt a sharp pain. But there in front of her stood the handsome young Prince. He stared at her with his coal-black eyes, so that she cast down her own—and saw that her fish's tail had gone and she had the sweetest little white legs that any young girl could wish for; but she was quite naked, and so she wrapped herself in her long flowing hair. The Prince asked who she was and how she had come there, and she could only look back at him so gently and yet so sadly out of her deep-blue eyes; for of course she couldn't speak. Then he took her by the hand and led her into the castle. Every step she took, as the witch had foretold, was as though she were treading on sharp knives and pricking gimlets; but she gladly put up with that. By the side of the Prince she went along as lightly as a bubble; and he and all of them marveled at the charm of her graceful movements.

Costly dresses were given her of silk and muslin; she was the most beautiful in all the castle. But she was dumb; she could neither sing nor speak. Lovely slave-girls in gold and silk came out and danced before the Prince and his royal parents; one of them sang more beautifully than all the rest, and the Prince clapped his hands and smiled at her. This saddened the little mermaid, for she knew that she herself had sung far more beautifully. And she thought, "Oh, if only he knew that I gave my voice away forever, in order to be with him!"

Next, the slave-girls danced a graceful gliding dance to the most delightful music; and then the little mermaid raised her pretty white arms, lingered on the tips of her toes and then glided across the floor, dancing as no one had danced before. She looked more and more lovely with every movement, and her eyes spoke more deeply to the heart than the slave-girls' singing.

Everyone was enchanted, and especially the Prince, who called her his little foundling. Still she went on dancing, although every time her foot touched the ground it felt as though she was treading on sharp knives. The Prince said that she must never leave him, and she was allowed to sleep on a velvet cushion outside his door.

He had boys' clothes made for her, so that she could go riding with him on horseback. They rode through the sweet-smelling woods, where the green boughs grazed her shoulders and the little birds sang among the cool foliage. She went climbing with the Prince up high mountains and, although her delicate feet bled so that others could see it, she only laughed and went on and on with him, until they could see the clouds sailing below them like a flock of birds migrating to other lands.

Back at the Prince's castle, when at night the others were asleep, she would go out on to the broad marble steps and cool her tingling feet in the cold sea water; and then she would think of those down there in the depths of the sea.

One night her sisters rose up arm in arm, singing so mournfully as they swam on the water. She made signs to them, and they recognized her and told her how unhappy she had made them all. After that, they used to visit her every night; and once, in the far distance, she saw her old grandmother who hadn't been above the water for many years, and also the Sea King wearing his crown. They both stretched out their hands toward her, but they didn't venture in so near to the shore as the five sisters.

Day by day she became dearer to the Prince. He loved her as one loves a dear good child, but he didn't dream of making her his Queen; and yet she had to become his wife, or else she would never win an

immortal soul, but on his wedding morning would be turned to foam on the sea.

"Do you like me best of all?" the little mermaid's eyes seemed to say, when he took her in his arms and kissed her lovely brow.

"Yes," said the Prince, "you're the dearest of all, because you have the kindest heart. You are the most devoted to me, and you remind me of a young girl I once saw but shall probably never see again. I was sailing in a ship that was wrecked; the waves drove me ashore near a sacred temple where a number of young girls were serving. The youngest, who found me on the beach and saved my life—I only saw her twice. She was the only one I could ever love in this world, but you are so like her that you almost take the place of her image in my heart. She belongs to the holy temple, so that fortune has been kind in sending you to me. We will never part."

"Ah, little does he know that it was I who saved his life," thought the mermaid, "that I carried him across the sea to the temple in the wood, that I waited in the foam and watched if anyone would come. I saw the pretty girl he loves better than me"—and the mermaid sighed deeply, for she didn't know how to cry. "The girl belongs to the sacred temple, he says; she'll never come out into the world, and they'll never meet again. I am with him, I see him every day. I will take care of him, love him, give up my life to him."

But now the Prince was getting married, they said—married to the pretty daughter of the neighboring King, and that was why he was fitting out such a splendid ship. The Prince was going off to take a look at his neighbor's kingdom—that was how they put it, meaning that it was really to take a look at his neighbor's daughter. A large suite was to go with him, but the little mermaid shook her head and

laughed. She knew the Prince's thoughts far better than all the others. "I shall have to go," he had said to her. "I shall have to visit the pretty Princess, as my parents are so insistent. But force me to bring her back here as my wife, that they will never do. I can't love her. She's not like the beautiful girl in the temple, as you are. If I ever had to find a bride, I would rather have you, my dear mute foundling with the speaking eyes," and he kissed her red mouth, played with her long hair and laid his head against her heart, so that it dreamed of human happiness and an immortal soul.

"You've no fear of the sea, have you, my dumb child?" he asked, as they stood on board the splendid ship that was to take him to the neighboring kingdom. And he told her of stormy gales and dead calms, of strange fishes at the bottom of the ocean, and all that the diver had seen there; and she smiled at his tales, for she knew better than anyone else about the bottom of the sea.

At night, when there was an unclouded moon and all were asleep but the helmsman at his wheel, she sat by the ship's rail and stared down through the clear water; and she seemed to see her father's palace, with her old grandmother standing on the top of it in her silver crown and gazing up through the swift current at the keel of the vessel. Then her sisters came up on to the water and looked at her with eyes full of sorrow, wringing their white hands. She beckoned to them and smiled and would have liked to tell them that all was going well and happily with her; but the cabin boy came up at that moment, and the sisters dived down, so that the boy felt satisfied that the white something he had seen was foam on the water.

Next morning the ship sailed into the harbor of the neighboring King's magnificent capital. The church bells all rang out; and trumpets were blown from the tall battlements, while the soldiers saluted with gleaming bayonets and flying colors. Every day there was a fête. Balls and parties were given one after another, but nothing had yet been seen of the Princess; it was said that she was being educated abroad in a sacred temple, where she had lessons in all the royal virtues. At last she arrived.

The little mermaid was eager for a glimpse of her beauty, and she had to admit that she had never seen anyone more charming to look at. Her complexion was so clear and delicate, and behind the long dark lashes smiled a pair of trusting deep-blue eyes.

"It's you!" cried the Prince. "You who rescued me, when I was lying half-dead on the shore." And he clasped his blushing bride in his arms. "Oh, I'm too, too happy," he said to the little mermaid. "My dearest wish—more than I ever dared to hope for—has been granted me. My happiness will give you pleasure, because you're fonder of me than any of the others." Then the little mermaid kissed his hand, and already she felt as if her heart was breaking. The morrow of his wedding would mean death to her and change her to foam on the sea.

All the church bells were ringing, as the heralds rode round the streets to proclaim the betrothal. On every altar sweet oil was burning in rich lamps of silver. The priests swung their censers, and bride and bridegroom joined hands and received the blessing of the bishop.

Dressed in silk and gold, the little mermaid stood holding the bride's train; but her ears never heard the festive music, her eyes never saw the holy rites; she was thinking of her last night on earth, of all she had lost in this world.

That same evening, bride and bridegroom went on board the ship; the cannon thundered, the flags were all flying, and amidships they had put up a royal tent of gold and purple, strewn with luxurious cushions; here the wedded couple were to sleep that calm cool night.

The sails filled with the breeze and the ship glided lightly and smoothly over the clear water.

As darkness fell, colored lanterns were lit, and the crew danced merrily on the deck. The little mermaid could not help thinking of the first time she came up out of the sea and gazed on just such a scene of joy and splendor. And now she joined in the dance, swerving and swooping as lightly as a swallow that avoids pursuit; and shouts of admiration greeted her on every side. Never had she danced so brilliantly. It was as if sharp knives were wounding her delicate feet, but she never felt it; more painful was the wound in her heart. She knew that this was the last evening she would see the Prince for whom she had turned her back on kindred and home, given up her beautiful voice, and every day suffered hours of agony without his suspecting a thing. This was the last night she would breathe the same air as he, gaze on the deep sea and the star-blue sky. An endless night, without thoughts, without dreams, awaited her who had no soul and could never win one . . . All was joy and merriment on board until long past midnight. She laughed and danced with the thought of death in her heart. The Prince kissed his lovely bride, and she toyed with his dark hair, and arm in arm they went to rest in the magnificent tent.

The ship was now hushed and still; only the helmsman was there at his wheel. And the little mermaid leaned with her white arms on the rail and looked eastward for a sign of the pink dawn. The first ray of the sun, she knew, would kill her. Suddenly she saw her sisters rising out of the sea. They were pale, like her; no more was their beautiful long hair fluttering in the wind—it had been cut off.

"We have given it to the witch, so that she might help us to save you from dying when tonight is over. She has given us a knife—look, here it is—do you see how sharp it is? Before sunrise you must stab it into the Prince's heart. Then, when his warm blood splashes over your feet, they will grow together into a fish's tail, and you will become a mermaid once more; you will be able to come down to us in the water and live out your three hundred years before being changed into the dead salt foam of the sea. Make haste! Either he or you must die before the sun rises. Our old grandmother has been sorrowing till her white hair has fallen away, as ours fell before the witch's scissors. Kill the Prince and come back to us! But make haste—look at that red gleam in the sky. In a few minutes the sun will rise, and then you must die." And with a strange deep sigh they sank beneath the waves.

The little mermaid drew aside the purple curtain of the tent, and she saw the lovely bride sleeping with her head on the Prince's breast. She stooped and kissed his handsome brow, looked at the sky where the pink dawn glowed brighter and brighter, looked at the sharp knife in her hand, and again fixed her eyes on the Prince, who murmured in his dreams the name of his bride—she alone was in his thoughts. The knife quivered in the mermaid's hand—but then she flung it far out into the waves; they glimmered red where it fell, and what looked like drops of blood came oozing out of the water. With a last glance at the Prince from eyes half-dimmed in death she hurled herself from the ship into the sea and felt her body dissolving into foam.

And now the sun came rising from the sea. Its rays fell gentle and warm on the death-chilled foam, and the little mermaid had no feeling of death. She saw the bright sun and, hovering above her, hundreds of lovely creatures—she could see right through them, see the white sails of the ship and the pink clouds in the sky. And their voice was the voice of melody, yet so spiritual that no human ear could hear it, just as no earthly eye could see them. They had no wings, but their own lightness bore them up as they floated through the air. The little mermaid saw that she had a body like theirs, raising itself freer and freer from the foam.

"To whom am I coming?" she asked, and her voice sounded like that of the other beings, more spiritual than any earthly music can record.

"To the daughters of the air," answered the others. "A mermaid has no immortal soul and can never have one unless she wins the love of a mortal. Eternity, for her, depends on a power outside her. Neither have the daughters of the air an everlasting soul, but by good deeds they can shape one for themselves. We shall fly to the hot countries, where the stifling air of pestilence means death to mankind; we shall bring them cool breezes. We shall scatter the fragrance of flowers through the air and send them comfort and healing. When for three hundred years we have striven to do the good we can, then we shall win an immortal soul and have a share in mankind's eternal happiness. You, poor little mermaid, have striven for that with all your heart; you have suffered and endured, and have raised yourself into the world of the spirits of the air. Now, by three hundred years of good deeds, you too can shape for yourself an immortal soul."

And the little mermaid raised her crystal arms toward God's sun, and for the first time she knew the feeling of tears.

On board the ship there was bustle and life once more. She saw the Prince with his pretty bride looking about for her; sorrowfully they stared at the heaving foam, as if they knew she had thrown herself into the waves. Unseen, she kissed the forehead of the bride, gave a smile to the Prince, and then with the other children of the air she climbed to a rose-red cloud that was sailing in the sky.

"So we shall float for three hundred years, till at last we come into the heavenly kingdom."

"And we may reach it even sooner," whispered one. "Unseen we float into human homes where there are children and, for every day we find a good child who makes father and mother happy and earns their love, God shortens our time of trial. The child never knows when we fly through the room and, if that makes us smile with joy, then a year is taken away from the three hundred. But if we see a child who is naughty or spiteful, then we have to weep tears of sorrow, and every tear adds one more day to our time of trial."

The Emperor's New Clothes

Many years ago there lived an Emperor who was so tremendously fond of fine new clothes that he spent all his money on being elegantly dressed. He took no interest in his army or the theatre or in driving through the country, unless it was to show off his new clothes. He had different clothes for every hour of the day and, just as you might say of a King that he was in the council chamber, so it was always said of the Emperor: "He's in his wardrobe."

There was plenty of fun going on in the city where the Emperor lived. Strangers were continually arriving, and one day there came

two swindlers. They made out they were weavers and could weave the very finest stuffs imaginable. Not only were colors and design unusually attractive, but the clothes made from their material had the peculiarity of being invisible to anyone who wasn't fit for his post or who was hopelessly stupid.

"I say! They must be wonderful clothes," thought the Emperor. "If I had some, I could find out which of my statesmen were unfit for their posts and also be able to tell the clever ones from the stupid. Yes, I must have some of that stuff woven for me at once." And he paid down a large sum of money to the swindlers straight away, so as to enable them to start work.

And they did; they put up a couple of looms and pretended to be working, although there was absolutely nothing in the loom. They coolly demanded the most delicate silk and the finest gold thread, which they promptly stowed away in their own bags; and then they went on working far into the night at their empty looms.

"Well, now, I wonder how they are getting on with the work," said the Emperor to himself. But there was one point that really made him feel rather anxious, namely, that a man who was stupid or quite unfit for his post would never be able to see what was woven. Not that he need have any fears for himself—he was quite confident about that—but all the same it might be better to send someone else first, to find out how things were going. Everyone in the city had heard of the mysterious power possessed by the material, and they were all eager to discover how incapable or stupid their neighbors were.

"I'll send my honest old Prime Minister to the weavers," thought the Emperor. "He's the best one to see what the stuff looks like, for

he has plenty of sense and nobody fills his post better than he does."

So off went the honest old Premier to the workshop where the two swindlers sat busy at their empty looms. "Lor' bless my soul!" thought the Minister with eyes starting out of his head. "Why, I can't see anything!" But he was careful not to say so.

The two swindlers begged him to take a closer look—didn't he find the colors and design most attractive? They then pointed to the empty loom but, although the poor old Minister opened his eyes wider and wider, he couldn't see a thing; for there wasn't a thing to see. "Good Lord!" he thought, "Is it possible that I'm stupid? I never suspected that, and not a soul must hear of it. Can it be that I'm unfit for my post? No, it will never do for me to say that I can't see the material."

"Well, what do you think of it?" asked the one who pretended to be weaving.

"Oh, it's charming! Quite exquisite!" said the old Minister, looking through his spectacles. "What a pattern and what coloring! I shall certainly tell the Emperor how pleased I am with it."

"Ah, we're glad to hear that," said the swindlers, and they then gave details of the colors and the peculiar design. The old Minister listened carefully, so as to be able to repeat all this when he came back to the Emperor—which he duly did.

The swindlers now demanded more money, more silk and more gold thread, for these would be required for weaving. They put it all into their own pockets—not a thread came into the loom—while they went on working the empty frames as before.

By and by, the Emperor sent another honest official to see how the weaving was getting on and whether the stuff wouldn't soon be ready. The same thing happened to him as to the Minister: he looked and looked but, as nothing was there but the empty looms, he couldn't see anything.

"There, isn't it a handsome piece!" said the swindlers, as they pointed out the beauty of the design which wasn't there at all.

"I know I'm not stupid," thought the man, "so it must be my fine position I'm not fit for. Some people might think that rather funny, but I must take good care they don't get to hear of it." And then he praised the material which he couldn't see and assured them of his delight in its charming shades and its beautiful design. "Yes, it's quite exquisite," he said to the Emperor, when he got back.

The splendid material became the talk of the town. And now the Emperor himself said he must see it while it was still in the loom. Quite a throng of select people, including the two honest old officials who had been there already, went with him to where both the crafty swindlers were now weaving for all they were worth without the vestige of a thread.

"Look, isn't it magnificent!" said the two honest officials. "If Your Majesty will but glance—what a pattern, what coloring!" And they pointed to the empty loom, feeling certain that the others could see the material.

"What's this?" thought the Emperor. "I can't see anything—this is appalling! Am I stupid? Am I not fit to be Emperor? This is the most terrible thing that could happen to me ... Oh, it's quite wonderful," he said to them. "It has our most gracious approval." And he gave a satisfied nod, as he looked at the empty loom; he wasn't going to say that he couldn't see anything. All the courtiers who had come with him looked and looked, but they made no more of it than the rest had done. Still, they all said just what the Emperor said—"Oh, it's quite wonderful!"—and they advised him to have some clothes made from this splendid new material and to wear them for the first time in the grand procession that was shortly taking place. "Magnificent!" "Delightful!" "Superb!" were the comments that ran from mouth to mouth; everyone was so intensely pleased with it. On each of the swindlers the Emperor bestowed a knighthood, with a badge to wear in his buttonhole, and the title of Imperial Weaver.

On the eve of the procession the swindlers sat up all night with something like twenty lighted candles. People could see how busy they were finishing off the Emperor's new clothes. They pretended to take the stuff off the loom, they clipped away at the air with huge scissors, they worked at their needles without thread, and at last they announced: "There! The Emperor's clothes are ready!"

Then the Emperor, with his most distinguished gentlemen-in-waiting, went in person to the weavers, who each put out his arm just as if he were holding something and said: "Here are the breeches! Here is the robe! Here is the mantle!" And so on. "They are all as light as gossamer; you can hardly feel you have anything on— that's just the beauty of them."

"Yes, indeed," answered the gentlemen-in-waiting. But they couldn't see a thing, for there wasn't a thing to see.

"Now will Your Imperial Majesty be graciously pleased to take off your clothes?" said the swindlers. "Then we can fit you with the new ones, there in front of the big glass."

So the Emperor took off the clothes he was wearing, and the swindlers pretended to hand him each of the new garments they were supposed to have made, and they took him at the waist as if they were fastening something on . . . it was the train, and the Emperor turned and twisted in front of the looking-glass.

"Goodness! How well they suit your Majesty! What a wonderful fit!" they all exclaimed. "What a cut! What colors! What sumptuous robes!"

The Master of Ceremonies came in with an announcement. "The canopy to be carried above Your Majesty in the procession is waiting outside."

"All right, I'm ready," said the Emperor. "Aren't they a nice fit!" And he turned round once more in front of the glass, for he really had to make them think he was gazing at his fine clothes.

The chamberlains who were to carry the train groped about on the floor as if they were picking the train up; and, as they walked, they held out their hands, not daring to let it be thought that they couldn't see anything.

There marched the Emperor in the procession under the beautiful canopy, and everybody in the streets and at the windows said: "Goodness! The Emperor's new clothes are the finest he has ever had. What a wonderful train! What a perfect fit!" No one would let it be thought that he couldn't see anything, because that would have meant he wasn't fit for his job, or that he was very stupid. Never had the Emperor's clothes been such a success.

"But he hasn't got anything on!" said a little child. "Goodness gracious, do you hear what the little innocent says?" cried the father; and the child's remark was whispered from one to the other.

"He hasn't got anything on! There's a little child saying he hasn't got anything on!"

"Well, but he hasn't got anything on!" the people all shouted at last. And the Emperor felt most uncomfortable, for it seemed to him that the people were right. But somehow he thought to himself: "I must go through with it now, procession and all." And he drew himself up still more proudly, while his chamberlains walked after him carrying the train that wasn't there.

Simple Simon

Away in the country, in an old manor house, lived an old squire. He had two sons who were so clever that—well, the fact is they were too clever by half. They made up their minds to go and propose to the King's daughter; and they had a perfect right to do this, because she had announced that she would marry the man who she thought was best able to speak up for himself.

The two sons now spent a week in preparation. A week was all they were allowed; but it was quite long enough, for they had had a good education, and that is such a help. One of them knew the whole Latin dictionary off by heart, and also the local newspaper for the last three years, both backwards and forwards. The other son had learnt up all the by-laws of the city companies and the things every alderman is supposed to know; he thought this would help him to talk politics with the Princess; and, besides, he knew how to embroider braces, he was so very clever with his fingers.

"I shall win the Princess!" cried both of them; and so their father gave them each a beautiful horse. The brother who had learnt off the dictionary and the newspapers got a coal-black horse; and the one

who knew all about aldermen and could do embroidery got a milk-white horse; and then they smeared the corners of their mouths with cod-liver oil, so that the words would come out pat. All the servants were down in the courtyard to see them mount their horses, when just at that moment up came the third brother; for there were three of them, though nobody ever took count of the third, because he wasn't a scholar like the other two. They called him Simple Simon.

"Where are you two off to in that get-up?" he asked.

"We're going to Court, to talk our way into favor with the Princess. Haven't you heard the proclamation that's been read out all over the country?" And then they told him all about it.

"Gosh! I mustn't miss this!" said Simple Simon. But his brothers laughed at him and rode away.

"Dad, let me have a horse!" cried Simple Simon. "I do so feel like getting married. If she'll have me, she'll have me; and if she won't, then I'll marry her all the same."

"What nonsense!" said the father. "I've no horse for you. Why, you never open your mouth. But look at your brothers—they are splendid fellows."

"If I can't have a horse," said the boy, "then I'll ride the billy goat. It's my own, and it'll carry me all right, I know." Then he got astride the billy goat, dug his heels into its sides and dashed off down the road. Phew! What a rate they went! "Look out! Here we come!" yelled Simple Simon, and his cries went echoing after him.

But his brothers rode on ahead in complete silence. They never said a word, because they had to turn over in their minds all the clever remarks they were going to make. It had to be most cunningly worked out, I can tell you.

"Tally-ho!" shouted Simple Simon, "here we are! Look what I found on the road," and he showed them a dead crow he had picked up.

"You simpleton!" they said. "What are you going to do with that?"

"I shall give it to the Princess."

"Yes, do!" they answered, laughing as they rode on.

"Tally-ho! Here we are! Now look what I've found. You don't find that on the road every day."

The brothers turned round again to see what it was. "You simpleton!" they said. "Why, that's an old clog with the vamp missing. Is the Princess to have that as well?"

"Yes, of course," said Simple Simon; and his brothers only laughed at him and rode on till they were a long way ahead.

"Tally-ho! Here we are!" shouted Simon. "My word! This is getting better and better. Tally-ho! This is grand!"

"What have you found this time?" asked the brothers.

"Oh, it's too good for anything," said Simple Simon. "Won't she be pleased, the Princess!"

"Ugh!" said the brothers. "Why, it's mud straight out of the ditch."

"Yes, that's just what it is," said Simple Simon, "and the very finest sort, too; it slips right through your fingers." And he filled his pocket with the mud.

But his two brothers rode on as hard as they could go, and the result was that they drew up at the city gate a whole hour ahead of him and found the suitors being given numbers in the order of their arrival. They were made to stand in rows, six in each file, and so close together that they couldn't move their arms. This was just as well, for otherwise they might have stabbed each other in the back, just because one was in front of the other.

The rest of the inhabitants all crowded around the castle, right up against the windows, so as to watch the Princess receiving her suitors; but as soon as ever one of them came into her presence, he was completely tongue-tied. "No good!" the Princess kept saying. "Skedaddle!"

Now it was the turn of the brother who knew the dictionary by heart. But he had clean forgotten it while he was standing in the queue; and the floor creaked under him, and the ceiling was all covered with mirrors, so that he saw himself standing on his head. At the window stood three clerks and an alderman, who all wrote down every word that was spoken, so that it could go straight into the newspaper and be sold for a penny at the street corner. It was dreadful; and, what's more, they had made up such a fire that the stove was red hot.

"It's very warm in here," said the suitor.

"That's because my father's roasting cockerels today," said the Princess.

"O-o-oh!" was all he could say, as he stood there. He hadn't expected a remark like that, and he was hoping to say something witty. "O-o-oh!"

"No good!" said the Princess. "Skedaddle!"—and away he had to go. After that the second brother came in.

"It's dreadfully hot in here," he said.

"Yes, we're roasting cockerels for dinner," said the Princess.

"I b-beg your—b-beg your—" he stuttered; and the clerks all wrote down "I b-beg your—b-beg your—"

"No good!" said the Princess. "Skedaddle!"

105

Now it was Simple Simon's turn. He came trotting in on the billy goat, right into the palace-room. "Why, it's as hot as blazes in here!" he said.

"That's because I'm roasting cockerels," said the Princess.

"Oh, I say, that's lucky," said Simple Simon. "So I suppose I can have a crow roasted, can't I!"

"Of course you can, quite easily," said the Princess; "but have you got anything to roast it in, for I've neither pot nor pan."

"But I have," said Simon. "Here's a cooker with a tin handle!" And he produced the old clog and popped the crow straight into it.

"It will make quite a meal," said the Princess. "But what shall we do for gravy?"

"I've got that in my pocket," said Simon. "I've enough and to spare." And he tipped a little mud out of his pocket.

"I do like that!" said the Princess. "You know how to answer; you can speak up for yourself, and you're the one I'm going to marry! But do you realize that every word we've been saying has been written down and will be in the papers tomorrow? Look there

by the window—three clerks and an old alderman; and the alderman is the worst, because he doesn't understand a thing." Of course she said this just to frighten him. And the clerks all guffawed and made a great blot of ink on the floor.

"So these are the gentry?" said Simon. "Well, here's one for the alderman!" And he turned out his pocket and let him have the mud full in the face.

"Well done!" cried the Princess. "I could never have done that, but I'll soon learn."

So in the end Simple Simon became King, with a wife of his own and a crown and a throne. And all this comes straight out of the alderman's newspaper; so it may not be perfectly true!

It's Absolutely True

"It's a terrible affair!" said a hen—speaking, too, in quite another part of the town from where it all happened. "It's a terrible affair about that chicken house. I daren't sleep alone tonight. It's a good thing there are so many of us roosting together." And then she told them her story, which made the other hens' feathers stand on end and even set the cock's comb drooping. It's absolutely true!

But let's begin at the beginning. It was in a chicken house at the other end of the town. The sun went down, and the hens flew up. One of them was a white short-legged bird, who regularly laid her eggs and was altogether a most respectable hen. When she got to her perch she preened herself with her beak, and a little feather came out and went fluttering down. "So much for that one!" she said. "The more I preen, the lovelier I shall grow, no doubt!" Of course it was only said in fun, because she was the fun-maker among the hens, though in other ways (as you've just heard) most respectable. After that, she went off to sleep.

All about was quite dark; hen sat with hen, but the one next to her was still awake. She had heard, and had not heard—as you must often do in this world, if you are to live in peace and quiet. And yet she couldn't help saying to the hen perched on the other side of her, "Did you hear that? I give no names, but there is a hen who means

to pluck out her feathers for the sake of her looks. If I were a cock, I'd simply despise her."

Now directly above the hens sat the owl, with her owl husband and her owl children. They had sharp ears in that family; they could hear every word their hen neighbor said; and they rolled their eyes, and the owl mother fanned herself with her wings. "Don't take any notice—but of course you heard what she said, didn't you? I heard it with my own ears, and they're going to hear a lot before they drop off. One of the hens has so far forgotten what is fit and proper for a hen that she's calmly plucking out all her feathers in full view of the cock."

"Prenez garde aux enfants!" said the father owl. "Not in the children's hearing!"

"But I must tell the owl over the way; she's so highly respected in our set." And away flew the mother.

"Tu-whit, tu-who!" they both hooted, and it carried right down to the doves in the dove-cot across the yard. "Have you heard, have you heard? Tu-who! There's a hen that's plucked out all her feathers for the sake of the cock. She'll freeze to death, if she isn't dead already, tu-who!"

"Where, ooh, where?" cooed the doves.

"In the yard opposite. I as good as saw it with my own eyes. Really the story's almost too improper to repeat; but it's absolutely true."

"Tr-rue, tr-rue, every wor-rd!" said the doves; and they cooed down to their hen run, "There's a hen, some say there are two, who have plucked out all their feathers so as to look different from the others and to attract the attention of the cock. It's a risky thing to do; suppose they catch cold and die of fever . . . Yes, they're dead— two of them."

Then the cock joined in: "Wake up, wake up!" he crowed, and flew up on to the wooden fence. His eyes were still sleepy, but he crowed away all the same. "Three hens have died of love for a cock; they had plucked out all their feathers. It's a horrible story—I don't want it—pass it on!" "Pass it on!" squeaked the bats; and the hens clucked and the cocks crowed, "Pass it on, pass it on!" And so the story flew from one hen house to another, till at last it came back to the place where it had really started.

"There are five hens"—that's how it ran— "who have all plucked out their feathers to show which of them had got thinnest for love of the cock. Then they pecked at each other till the blood came and they all fell down dead, to the shame and disgrace of their family and the serious loss of their owner."

The hen that had lost the one loose little feather didn't of course recognize her own story and, as she was a respectable hen, she said, "How I despise those hens!—though there are plenty more just like them. That's not the kind of thing to be hushed up, and I shall do my best to get the story into the papers, so that it may go all over the country. It'll serve those hens right, and their families too."

And into the papers it came—all there in print—and it's absolutely true: "One little feather can easily become five hens!"